# Little and Big

Anne Gutman & Georg Hallensleben

Hippo Park

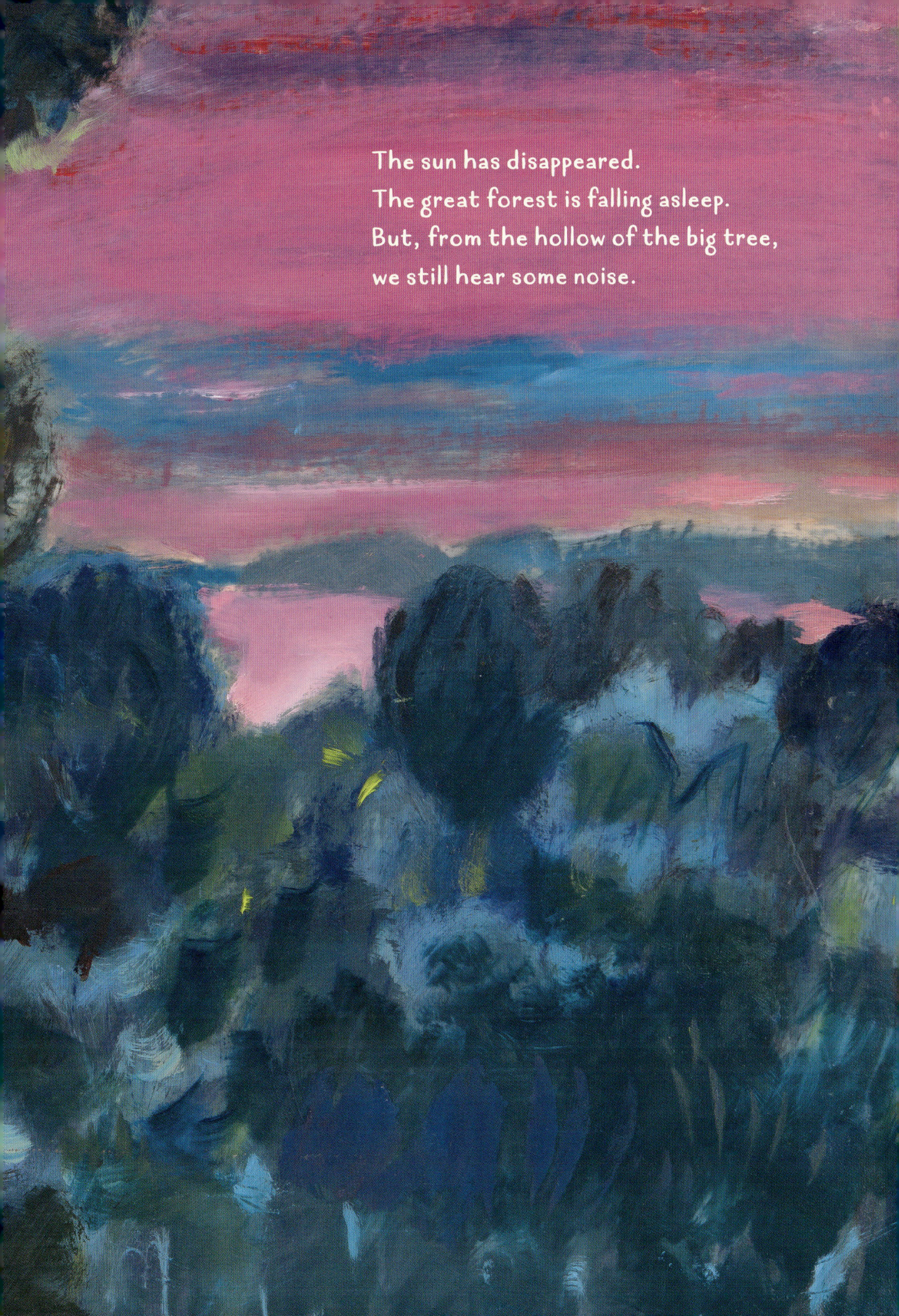

The sun has disappeared.
The great forest is falling asleep.
But, from the hollow of the big tree,
we still hear some noise.

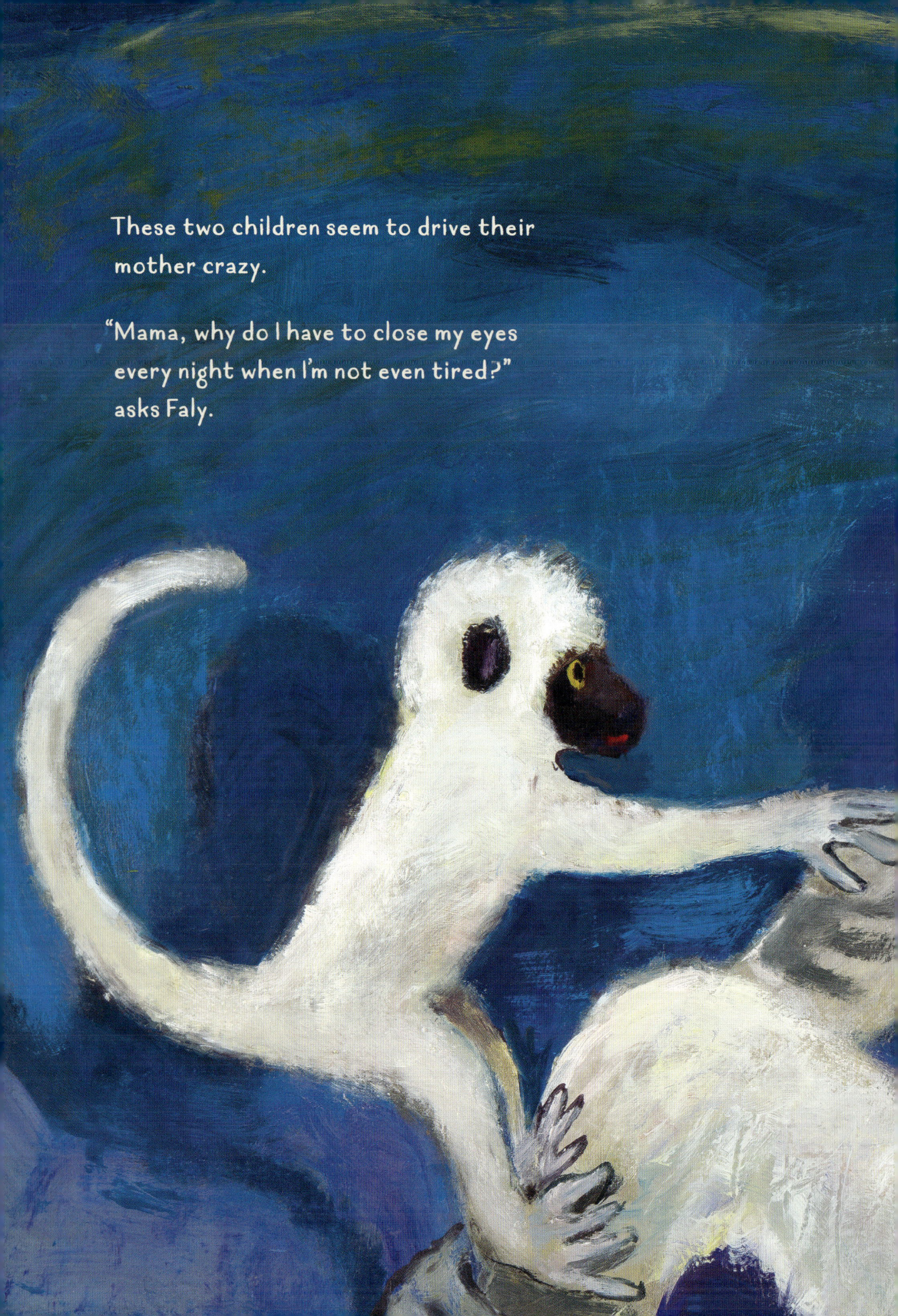

These two children seem to drive their mother crazy.

"Mama, why do I have to close my eyes every night when I'm not even tired?" asks Faly.

"Because it's time to go to sleep, Faly," Mama says.

"Well, I'm only going to sleep if Mahandry does, too!" protests Faly.

"But, Faly," Mahandry says. "I am allowed to stay up later because I'm big."

"I would like to be big, too . . . ," Faly murmurs.

After a short night, the children were up at dawn. As the jungle awakens, Faly and Mahandry swing from the tree, ready for adventure.

"Quick, climb on my back, Faly," says Mama. "We want to get to the river before the sun is too high."

"Move over, Faly!" Mahandry yells. "There's no room left for me!"

"Mahandry, you're too big," Mama says, laughing. "If I carried you like I used to, I'd get flattened like a pancake!"

"I wish I were still little . . . ," Mahandry murmurs.

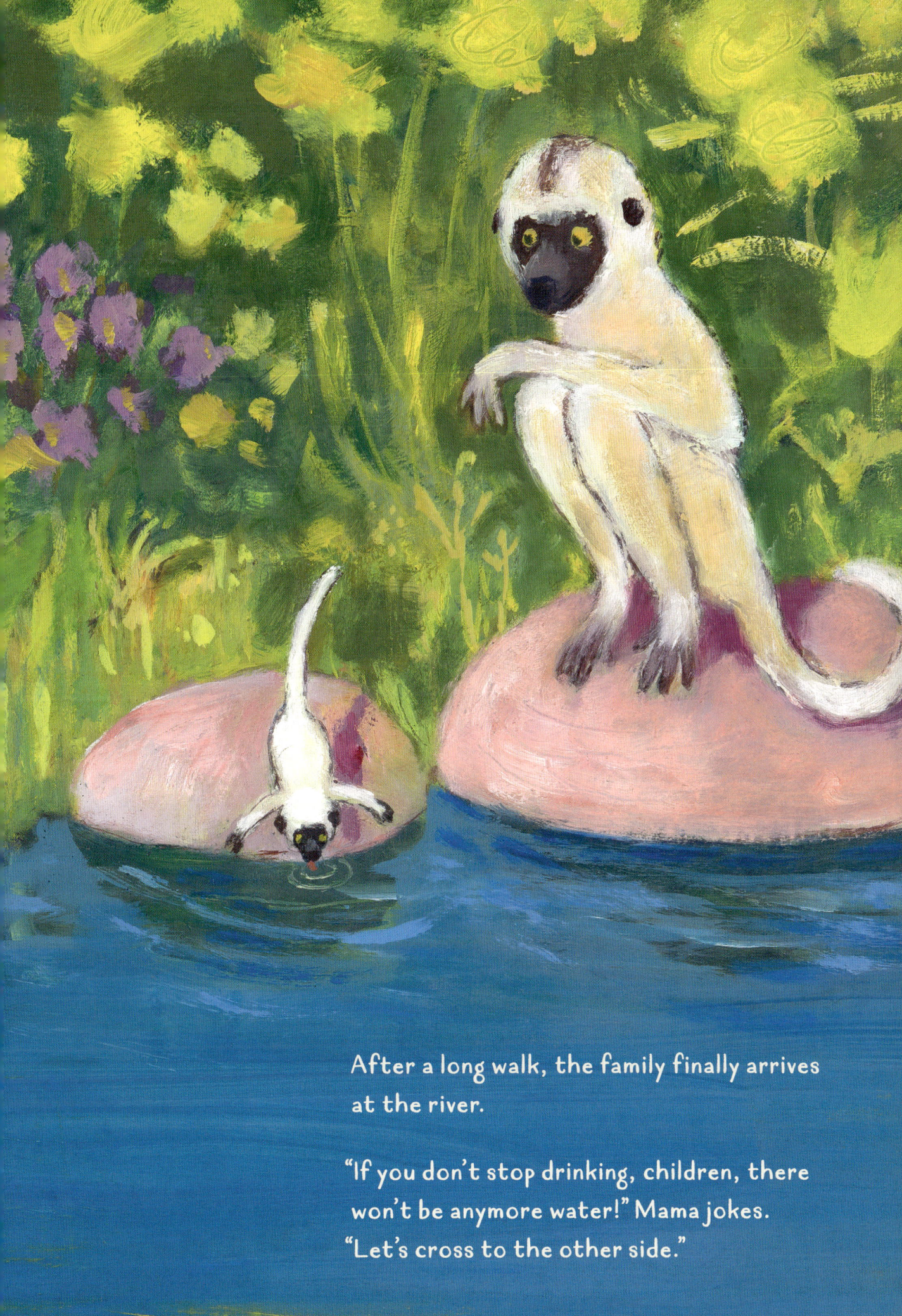

After a long walk, the family finally arrives at the river.

"If you don't stop drinking, children, there won't be anymore water!" Mama jokes. "Let's cross to the other side."

"The water here is too deep, even for a giraffe," Faly says with worry. "How are we going to make it, Mama?"

"It's easy. Watch me," says Mahandry. "Just be careful, the moss is slippery!" But Mama holds Faly back. He is too little to jump from stone to stone by himself.

"I wish I were big, too . . . ," Faly murmurs.

Mahandry and Faly run toward the big waterfall. "Stay close to me," Mama says, "this is not a good place to play. The rapids could pull you to the other side of the island!"

Faly jumps into his mama's arms and clings to her neck. But Mahandry must cross by himself. He doesn't feel very confident.

"Don't be afraid, my brave Mahandry," Mama says. "Just follow closely behind us!"

"I wish I were still little, too . . . ," Mahandry murmurs.

"I'm going to dry off on the branch," Mahandry says.

"You climbed way too high, Mahandry," Faly complains. "I can't see you anymore!"

"I can see the whole jungle from up here! I see beyond the big trees. I even see the herd of hippos!" cries Mahandry.

"I wish I were big, too . . . ," Faly murmurs.

Mahandry and Faly haven't eaten yet today.
Mama knows where to find the best lychees.
She offers to peel some for Faly.

"If only I were still little . . . I don't like peeling the skin off, either," Mahandry murmurs.

"Well, I'm going to see if I can find a chameleon to nibble on," Mahandry says.

Up jumps Faly. He wants to go, too. But Mama says no. Faly is still too young for this kind of adventure.

"I wish I were big," whispers Faly, "so I could have a little fun, too..."

The chameleon hunt was not very good, but Mahandry discovers a path covered with beautiful orchids!

"These are the most delicious flowers I've ever tasted," Mahandry mumbles with his mouth full. "Try one, Faly!"

Mama helps Faly climb on her shoulders so he can pick the flowers himself.

"The higher ones smell even sweeter!" cries Faly.

"I wish I were still little. Then Mama would help me too . . . ," Mahandry murmurs.

"We've eaten enough, my little gluttons," says Mama. "Let's get home before dark."

"But the moths and bats haven't even come out yet," protests Mahandry. "I love nighttime adventures . . ."

"The darkness is full of new dangers for you, Faly," says Mama. "You're not yet as skillfull and quick as Mahandry."

"I would like to be big, too . . . ," Faly murmurs.

The sun has disappeared. Little by little, the forest is falling asleep. And, in the hollow of the big tree, everything is quiet.

Faly lets his head fall back on the pillow of leaves. It is time to sleep.

"I'm sleepy, too," says Mahandry. "Can we snuggle up close like we used to, Mama?"

Mama gathers Faly and Mahandry in her arms.

"Go to sleep, my children," she whispers. "Tomorrow, you will both wake up a little bigger than you are today. But you will always be my little ones. My sweet little ones."

To our son, Robinson

Text copyright © 2024 by Anne Gutman
Illustrations copyright © 2024 by Georg Hallensleben
Translated from French by Jill Davis
All rights reserved. Copying or digitizing this book for storage, display,
or distribution in any other medium is strictly prohibited.
For information about permission to reproduce selections from this book,
please contact permissions@astrapublishinghouse.com.

 Hippo Park

Hippo Park
An imprint of Astra Books for Young Readers,
a division of Astra Publishing House
astrapublishinghouse.com
Printed in China

ISBN: 978-1-6626-4048-3 (hc)

ISBN: 978-1-6626-4049-0 (eBook)
Library of Congress Control Number: 2023905113

First edition

10 9 8 7 6 5 4 3 2 1

Design by Melia Parsloe
The text is set in Quimbly.
The titles are handlettered by Georg Hallensleben.
The illustrations are done in oil paint.